MW00939125

THE
MONSTERS
OF
MARYMOUNT
MANSION

The Monsters of Marymount Mansion

by Gregory G. Allen

For All Those Monsters
Who are Hiding

The Monsters of Marymount Mansion

Copyright © 2023 Gregory G. Allen All rights reserved

ASD Publishing

ISBN: 978-0-9961029-4-0

Library of Congress Control Number: 2023940040

Book Design by Shelby Goodwin

Manufactured in the United States of America

www.asdmedia.co

Table of Contents

PROLOGUE

"Toby, wake up," he heard his mother saying.

Had he really been asleep that long? He felt like he had just seen the moon rise high in the October sky from the small window where he could watch the outside world. When you lived with strict rules the way that he did, the days would all run together and nighttime would go by too quickly. He often found himself very bored.

"What eight-year-old should have to live this way?" he asked anyone who would listen.

But no response came. Just the sound of his own voice echoing off the musty walls after his mom had left him.

Toby tried to think of something that could bring him happiness for the day. It was October, and October meant one of his favorite holidays.

Halloween.

1

The House on the Hill

Fall was in the air around the historic mansion at the top of the hill in the small town of Reddington. Celeste Marymount and her staff, married couple Rick and Margaret Harley, were hanging up Halloween decorations around the mansion, which had been passed down through generations of Marymounts before her. Even though she had very few guests, it was always important that the place be fully decorated for each holiday.

"Sometimes I think I'm getting too old for this," Celeste said.

"Being in your seventies isn't old," Rick replied.

"Tell that to my niece and nephew."

"We haven't seen them in so long," Margaret said as she hung bat wings around the fireplace.

"Those two are older with families of their own," Celeste said. "They take after their dad and don't care about making it back to their family home."

"We care," Rick announced.

"And I appreciate it," Celeste said. "Sometimes I think you two are more like my family than my actual family."

"Family is what you make of it," Margaret observed. "We are chosen family."

"I like that," Celeste said.

Family had always been important to Celeste. It was the generations before her that opened the mansion to the public as a place for people to spend the night and wake to a delicious home-cooked meal. Guests were greeted each morning by the smell of biscuits and gravy with sizzling sausage in the pan the moment the neighboring rooster woke them with its vocal alarm. Famous celebrities and politicians had found rest in the rooms of this very cozy home for years. But as the town of Reddington changed and new highways didn't lead to downtown, the number of customers had dwindled.

Now the mansion was lucky to get a few guests throughout the year.

"I need to get out on that porch and fix some of those creaky boards this weekend," Rick said.

"I don't know," Margaret chimed in. "It sort of adds to the spooky house on the hill feel to the season."

She turned on some music, and the three laughed and danced around the room. Celeste let out a "Boooooo," giving her best ghost impersonation. Suddenly there was a creak from the basement door down the hallway…as if someone was turning the doorknob.

"Did anyone hear that?" Margaret asked, wide-eyed.

"I didn't hear anything," Celeste said.

"Must have been the wind," Margaret uttered, glancing around.

"You are always hearing noises in this old house," Rick interjected.

"You can't help it," Celeste said. "The noises are all part of being in a hundred-and-fifty-year-old home. So, where should we put these jack-'o-lanterns?"

The subject successfully changed, the other two went back to putting up Halloween decorations while Celeste headed to the kitchen to bake some cookies. Even though there were no paying guests at the moment, there were others in the house who loved the smell of baking cookies.

Celeste had often thought of sharing her secret with Margaret and Rick, but wasn't sure how they would take it. She had been sitting on this mysterious information for decades. She had never even told anyone in her family the secret of Marymount Mansion. No one else knew about the monsters who lived in the basement.

That's right. Celeste wasn't alone, as she always had company living beneath her. It had been her idea several decades before to allow the monsters to come upstairs when she would throw big Halloween parties. They loved that they could mingle with her guests as everyone thought they were dressed up for the occasion. The guests would come as witches, mummies, and vampires, and the monsters would fit right in...sometimes winning the best-costume contest at the end of the night.

Through the years, Celeste had become close with the monsters. She was never frightened of them. They had their own families and carried about their business in the basement. She would see to it that they had food, and they all looked forward to the one night of the year when they could come out of the basement and join the townspeople. She had witnessed monster weddings and monster births. She felt as if they were extra family members. Celeste was lucky to have the monsters of Marymount, and she believed they felt lucky for having her.

"Hold up your end on that cobweb,"

she heard Margaret say to Rick down the hall. The two worked just as hard as she did to get the place ready.

There was one particular monster that she knew loved Halloween, and she looked at him as if he was her own grandchild. Toby. She was there when Toby was born and had watched him take his first steps, speak for the first time, and read his first book. Toby did everything other little boys and girls did. If it wasn't for the fact that he was a monster, Celeste believed he could have gone to school and become a very smart child.

But Toby was different from the children

in town. He looked different, with his furry green skin that felt something like a cross between a fish's and a dog's. He sounded different, because his accent wasn't always the same as humans'. He smelled different, which wasn't a bad thing since he smelled like cotton candy. Whenever Toby got nervous or excited, he would let off a huge cloud of the sugary stuff.

Celeste knew it had been Toby trying to come upstairs earlier. He always wanted to get out of the basement. The closer they got to Halloween, the more excited and impatient he would become.

"We're heading out now," Rick announced, standing in the kitchen doorway.

"The day goes by so quickly with your help. You two have a wonderful evening at home," Celeste said.

"You too. Enjoy the stillness of the mansion."

"We will see you tomorrow," Margaret added as they went outside.

The sun was starting to go down, and Celeste watched as Rick and Margaret's car drove away. She locked the front door, dimmed the lights in the big, spacious house, and went to the kitchen to pick up the plate of cookies. She made her way down the long hallway to the large door that separated her from the basement-dwellers. The door opened with a creak and she slowly started down the steps.

"Toby. I know that was you earlier, trying to get upstairs," Celeste called. "Come out of those shadows and talk to me."

2

Toby's Surprise

Toby loved the smell of Ms. Celeste's cookies, but he didn't want to go anywhere near her this time. He knew Ms. Margaret and Mr. Rick had been upstairs and he shouldn't have tried to open the door earlier during the day. Ms. Celeste had always been kind to him and his family, and he was pushing her by trying to get out of the basement. But he *really* wanted to go upstairs and run around the mansion. He had played hide-and-seek once and found the big rooms to be so much fun. The basement was dark and dank and not as roomy as the rest of the house. Just getting upstairs meant having some elbow room and getting away from the other monsters in the basement, especially his little sister, Micaela, who always pestered him.

"Toby. We need to talk," Celeste said again.

"You heard her," Toby's mom said,

pulling on one of his many fingers. “Ms. Celeste isn’t playing around. Go own up to what you did.”

Toby walked toward the staircase with his mom, tiptoeing out of the shadows. Ms. Celeste had a stern look on her face and he didn’t like to be in trouble. His nerves caused a cloud of cotton candy smell to seep from his body. He also really wanted one of those cookies.

"Hello, Ms. Celeste," he said shyly.

"You don't need to be scared of me, Toby. I'm not going to bite," she replied.

"What do you say to Ms. Celeste?" Toby's mom asked.

"I'm sorry, Ms. Celeste," Toby said. "I know I'm not supposed to go upstairs. I just saw the date on the calendar, and I know Halloween is getting closer and closer."

"I know, Toby," she replied. "It's really hard to contain one's excitement, and you will get to come upstairs this year and you might even be allowed to go outside."

"What?" he yelled.

"Yes. I was talking to your mother, and we think this might be the year you can go out with the trick-or-treaters and see what it's like."

"Oh, Ms. Celeste...I'm so delighted!" he exclaimed.

"But you have to follow the rules," Celeste said. "And one of those is to stay in the basement, especially when you know someone else is in the mansion."

"I understand," he said. "I'm really sorry I tried to open that door. I didn't go through it though. I just stood at the top of the stairs and listened to the music Ms. Margaret was playing."

"Do you like music?" she asked.

"Oh, very much. I like all kinds of music that I hear coming downstairs."

"If you are good and promise to stay out of trouble, perhaps I can get you a radio. You will just need to play it softly."

"I can do that," Toby said.

"Very well. Please share this plate of cookies with the others," she said, handing it to him.

"Ms. Celeste, what's trick or treat?" he asked.

"Children go to houses, say 'trick or treat,' and ask for candy. People give them candy, or they might get a trick if they're not given a treat," she replied with a smile.

"Wow...candy."

"I will see you again tomorrow," Celeste said.

"Goodnight, Ms. Celeste."

"Goodnight, Toby."

And with that, Celeste disappeared back upstairs.

Toby couldn't believe he might get his own radio for the basement. He would be able to listen to music as well as humans talking about what was happening in the world. He always wondered what went on outside of Marymount Mansion. What did people do all day? Was it any different from his life in a smelly old basement? Toby had so many questions and hoped the radio people might be able to give him some answers.

The next day Toby woke up and went to the top of the staircase. He didn't touch the door. He wasn't going to do that again, but he did want to listen. He sat on the top step with his little green ear pushed to the door. He could hear Ms. Margaret and Mr. Rick at work, moving about the mansion.

"Yes, it will just be for one night," a man's voice boomed.

It sounded like someone was checking in. He always loved when there were other people in the house besides Ms. Celeste. Sometimes he could hear conversations through the vents from each room. The voices would carry all the way down to the basement, and it felt like he was listening to television or the radio.

Radio!

Ms. Celeste said he might be getting a radio. He wondered if it would play Halloween music. That was the only holiday he had really experienced. He couldn't wait for Halloween night and to finally go outside. He knew that was going to be a treat, even though Ms. Celeste said it was tricks as well.

Toby ran to the calendar to count the days. He only had to wait five more and then he would be free of the basement, at least for a night. Would outside people treat him the same way Ms. Celeste did? He knew he was different, and that was why they had to stay in the basement.

But each Halloween, no one could ever tell he was different when they joined the party upstairs. Maybe the outside people would be the same and see his skin as a costume. It made him giggle to think that he would be able to play that trick on people. Oh…that's what Ms. Celeste meant by "trick." He would be the trick and going outside would be the treat. His thoughts were interrupted when he saw Ms. Celeste coming down the staircase with a box in her hand.

3

Trick or Treat

It had been five days since Ms. Celeste had given Toby his gift, and he loved listening to his radio. He would sit in the corner of the basement for hours, listening to the way the people would talk and all the different kinds of music they would play. Sometimes he would get up and dance to it—at least, it felt like dancing from what he had seen at Halloween parties.

Halloween!

Wait, no one had mentioned the date. Toby ran to the calendar, and sure enough, it was October 31st. This was the big day. He had been told that once kids get out of school, they go out into the neighborhood asking people for candy. He felt like it was a little odd to ask people for stuff, but he figured why not do what the others were doing.

"I don't understand why I can't go outside with you," Micaela exclaimed.

"Because you're not eight years old yet," Toby told her. "When you're bigger you can join me. Just not this year."

"It's not fair," she yelled. "I want to see the kids dressed up too."

"I'll tell you all about it when I get back."

Toby went to the window, which was high up in the basement wall. He could see outside and would know when the sun was starting to go down. When the door opened, he bolted toward it.

“Goodbye, everyone!” Toby yelled. “I’ll bring you back some candy.”

Toby darted up the stairs. Ms. Celeste, who was waiting at the top, gave him a big hug along with a bag and walked him to the door.

“Now remember, if anyone tries to pull at your body thinking it’s a costume, just tell them it’s on really tightly.”

“I will, Ms. Celeste. Thank you.”

“And don’t let anyone scare you. Come right back home when you see the others heading toward their houses.” Toby ran out the door and stopped to smell the air. It felt amazing to be outside.

He couldn't compare it to anything else he had experienced. He saw kids dressed as all sort of things walking with bags, knocking on doors, and saying, "Trick or treat!" He decided to join them.

A kid rang the bell at the next house. The noise made Toby so nervous that he farted. Oops.

"Why do I smell cotton candy?" a kid dressed as a witch asked.

"I smell it too," exclaimed a vampire.

Toby tried to play off the fact that his body would ooze sugariness when he was anxious.

"Maybe they are cooking something

sweet in this house," he said.

The door opened and the kids all yelled "trick or treat." They were handed candy for their bags. Toby pushed his out and beamed when the treat was dropped inside.

"This is really neat," he shouted.

"Haven't you ever done this before?" the witch asked.

"This is my first time," he replied.

"You have a very cool costume," she said, touching his arm.

"Thanks."

"Come on! Let's hit the next house!" the vampire yelled.

Toby ran around the neighborhood with the kids for what felt like forever. It was great to be around others his age. He also felt accepted as everyone was in costumes and he fit in with the humans.

At the end of the night, his bag was full of candy, he had talked and laughed with the kids, and it was time to go home.

"Where do you live, Toby?" the witch asked.

"The big mansion up the hill."

"You live in Marymount Mansion? Wow," the vampire interjected.

"How come we never see you at school?" asked a mummy.

Toby was getting nervous. He felt he had shared too much.

"Umm...I'm just visiting the woman who lives there. I don't actually live with her. I'm from out of town," he said.

"That makes sense," replied the witch. "Hope to see you again. Bye."

The kids made their way down the street and Toby headed up toward the house. *That wasn't that hard*, he thought. *Why can't I do this other times?*

When he got home, Celeste was waiting at the door.

"How was it? Did you have a good time?" she asked.

"It was amazing, they were all so gracious. And I got candy for everyone."

"I'm so glad you got to experience this, Toby," she said as she walked him toward the basement. "This is something special you can look forward to each year."

Downstairs, Toby was rushed by all the other monsters, many asking him questions, many reaching for the candy.

"Candy!" Micaela shouted as she grabbed some, then took it to a corner of the basement.

Toby looked around and saw how overjoyed everyone was. What if he could make them this happy on more than one day a year? He had expected bullying and mean kids out in the world, but everything seemed great. Maybe he wouldn't wait a year until Halloween to go out again. He would try it on the next holiday.

4

Watch Those Feathers

The mansion smelled of pumpkin pies, turkey roasting in the oven, and fresh bread. There were a few guests staying for Thanksgiving and Celeste wanted them to feel like they were home with family. Downstairs was a completely different story. The monsters would wait until the humans were done eating upstairs before they could enjoy their own feast. Celeste would ring the bell when it was time for them to move about.

"Shhhhh," Mrs. Vanderpang said, standing still as a statue. She was an older monster who had lived with Toby's family for years. She was skinny and fluffy with

pink straw for hair. She had no children of her own and loved to tell Toby and Micaela what to do. Everyone froze as the humans moved about over their heads.

"Children, you must be extra quiet today," Toby's mom said. "Ms. Celeste has people upstairs."

"Ugh, I hate staying quiet all day," Micaela whined.

"Young monster, you will do as you're told. It's the least we can do for the woman who takes care of us," Toby's dad declared as Mrs. Vanderpang smiled knowingly.

Toby made a face at his little sister. The family would now be watching her, and he could sneak away to the top of the staircase. He placed his head against the door to listen to the conversations.

"I think we're in for a mild winter," one male voice said.

"I'm not so sure," another replied. "I've heard certain parts of the country are going to be covered in snow by December."

Toby wasn't sure why adults always talked about the weather, but figured while Ms. Celeste was busy with the guests, he would sneak outside and walk around.

He had heard on his radio about a parade happening in town that morning.

He had spent days creating a costume that resembled a turkey. He made big feathers to cover his fish-like skin. People would assume he was part of the parade while he witnessed what a Thanksgiving Day was all about.

The conversation seemed to be getting louder, so he knew it was time to make a break for it.

"Where are you going?" his little sister

said from behind him.

"Micaela," he whispered. "Go play in your corner."

"I'll tell," she yell-whispered.

"Don't say anything and I'll bring you something back."

"You're going outside again?"

"Shhhhh, you're too loud,"Toby warned. "I won't be long. I'm going to check out the parade."

"What's in your bag?" she asked.

"A costume."

"Why?"

"I can't go out as myself since it's not Halloween. So I'm dressing like a turkey."

"What if someone wants to eat you?" she asked.

"No one is going to eat me, silly."

"They eat turkey on this day all the time."

"Just go play, quietly," Toby said. "And don't tell Mom or Dad."

"Okay. Be careful."

"I will."

Toby slowly opened the door and tiptoed out of the mansion. In the backyard, he put on his turkey costume with all the bright feathers and headed toward Main Street, where he had heard the parade would take place.

There were so many people. Much more than on Halloween. He was overwhelmed by all the bodies and the noise. He kept bumping into people with his big feathers.

"Hey, watch those feathers, little boy!" someone shouted.

"Yes, sir," he said.

Toby was pleased that someone thought he was a little boy. They weren't even noticing that he was different. That he was actually a monster. He chuckled to himself.

With a bit more confidence, he decided

to walk along inside the parade. The streets were lined with people watching the floats. There were so many humans all up and down the road. Toby saw how people were waving, so he waved back.

"Look at that big turkey!" a little girl shouted.

"Oh, he's cute," the mom replied.

Toby beamed with pride. He did some of his dance steps as he marched down Main Street. Toby was so joyful he had decided to come out and witness this day. People really seemed to be cheerful and thankful, and he assumed that was what it was all about.

He watched as families gathered up to leave and go home to celebrate around their tables, where he was sure they had the same food he smelled at the mansion. As he walked home, he saw some kids playing football with their dads on a field. Everyone always seemed so pleased out in the real world. There were times in the basement that the monsters seemed happy too, but none of them knew what they were missing outside. There was so much more to experience, and staying hidden away didn't feel like a way to live.

Toby wondered if he would ever be able to live in the real world or if he would always be confined to the basement. Ms. Celeste was a wonderful host to all the monsters, but how long could she keep them hidden? What if someone found out? What if she moved away? Wouldn't it be better to just go out and take their chances? From what he'd seen, he didn't believe people would be mean to him. Maybe they would even grow to love the monsters.

Maybe he should give another holiday a try. When he listened to his radio, it seemed that people were most gleeful around holiday times. He had seen Santa appear at the end of the parade today. He had also heard the radio people talking about Christmas a lot. He figured he had a month to learn as much as he could. At eight years old he had already seen how Ms. Celeste had decorated the mansion for Christmas on previous years. This would be the year he would venture out and see what happened outside of the mansion on that special day.

The only question was what he would dress up as this time.

5

Cookies in the Basement

Snow was falling and lights were twinkling outside the frosted basement window. It was going to be a very cold Christmas holiday. Ms. Celeste had the entire mansion decorated in red and green. She had brought the monsters upstairs to see when no one had been around. Now there were guests, a fire roaring in the library fireplace, and the smell of cookies and desserts baking all throughout the day.

Toby loved this time of year. Ms. Celeste was always extra peppy and even kinder to the monsters…if that was possible, as she was normally a very kind woman. The previous week, she had put up a fake tree in the basement for the monsters to enjoy the holiday as well. Micaela loved decorating it and then re-decorating it. Toby had been working on a costume for his next great escape outside the mansion.

"I don't know how you keep getting away with it," Micaela declared.

"Because you've been a good sister and not told," Toby replied.

"Maybe you could bring me back a Christmas present this time."

"Micaela, I don't have any money. How would I get a present?"

"Ask Santa."

"I don't think Santa helps monster kids," Toby said. "We have a Santa's helper in Ms. Celeste."

"She is really good to us, but it would be nice to have a doll to play with," Micaela replied.

"Let me see what I can do."

Toby had no idea how he could get Micaela a doll, but figured he could get her to stop talking by saying he would try. He played Christmas music on his radio while the monsters laughed and talked about past holidays. It was swell spending time with his huge family in the basement, but Toby really wanted to expand his group of friends beyond the mansion walls.

He heard the basement door open, and Ms. Celeste walked down the stairs.

"Christmas cookies!" Micaela shouted, running toward her.

"I also have milk to go with them," Celeste announced. "You all need some of the Christmas spirit down here too."

"Maybe some of us older ones want a

cookie as well," Mrs. Vanderpang said as she reached for one. "Don't forget your elders."

"Ms. Celeste, you are too good to us," Toby's mom interjected.

"I count you all as family," Celeste replied. "I don't get to see mine much and I'm happy to have all of you in my life...in my home."

"We are very lucky to have you," Toby's mom said. "There aren't too many humans who would accept us the way you do."

"I've gotten used to the cotton candy smell," Celeste said. "I enjoy spending time with you all."

"So your brother won't be coming for this Christmas?" Toby's mom asked.

"Looks like he'll be staying away from the mansion again this year," Celeste said.

"At least you have family," Mrs. Vanderpang chimed in. "All of mine are gone."

"Mrs. Vanderpang, you know we view you as family," Toby's mom said.

"That's because you feel stuck with me."

Micaela jumped in with an idea.

"Then Ms. Celeste will just have to come downstairs and be with us," she announced.

Toby shot Micaela a look. How could she invite Ms. Celeste downstairs when she knew he was planning on sneaking out again? Micaela smiled a huge grin toward her brother.

"Ms. Celeste, have you ever wondered what it would be like if we could all go out into the world?" Micaela asked.

Why? Why is she going down this road with Ms. Celeste? Toby wondered. Micaela must have forgotten that Toby was going to try and find her a doll when he was outside.

"Well, Micaela, sometimes people don't like to be around those who are not exactly like them," Celeste said. "If you all went out in the world, I just don't know how folks would react, and I wouldn't want you to take that risk."

"Yeah...I bet it's a scary place out there," Micaela said, looking at Toby.

Now he knew his sister was just messing with him. She was pushing buttons to see how far she could go without giving away Toby's entire plan.

"You don't need to worry about it, Micaela," Celeste said. "You are safe down here."

"Yeah, Micaela," Toby said as he ate a Christmas cookie. "We have everything we need right here."

"I'm going to leave this whole plate and pitcher of milk for you all. Enjoy," Celeste said as she went back upstairs.

Toby's dad gathered the monsters around the tree, where they shared stories. His mom smiled and placed a big Christmas bow on top of Mrs. Vanderpang's pink head.

"How many Christmas Eves have monsters had in this

basement?" Micaela asked her dad.

"That's a tough question, Micaela, as none of us have been here the whole time," Dad said.

"The only person who could answer that question is Gwynasiam," Mrs. Vanderpang added.

No one spoke of Gwynasiam that much in the basement, but Toby had heard the name now and again. A wise old monster who lived somewhere else underneath the house. Toby lay down on the floor under the Christmas tree. He looked up at the twinkling lights and pretended they were stars far away in the sky. He imagined himself flying to one of those stars and starting a new life there. Maybe star people didn't mind if your skin was green or orange or blue and if you smelled different. Maybe there was a place far beyond Reddington, even beyond this country, that would accept him. Only way to find out was to get out there and try again. He had been out two times now, and he really wanted more.

6

The Elf with Horns

The air was crisp and the stars shone bright in the sky. Toby could hear the voices singing like a choir before he even saw them. Once he came around the corner of Peach Street, there the people were, standing in front of someone's house singing the most beautiful music.

"What amazing carols," the person standing in the door said. "Thank you for stopping by our house."

Were these the same houses that had given him candy at Halloween? And now people came back and sang to them to thank them for the candy?

He wasn't sure what was going on, but he liked this Christmas event. The person at the door gave the singers hot cider, which he could smell. It was like apples and cinnamon. Toby stood and smiled as the smell made its way up his nose. He then noticed the entire choir walking to another house and starting up the music again. More people would come out from each house, stand and listen, and then give them cookies or sweets.

I need to get in on this deal, he thought.

Just then, one of the kids turned and saw Toby.

"Look at that elf," they shouted,

pointing at him.

Toby had hoped his costume would keep him hidden for Christmas.

“He looks like a mixture of an elf and an animal,” another kid said, laughing.

“Yeah…I don’t recognize that character,” a third kid replied.

Toby wondered what he had done wrong with his costume. Feeling weird about it, he turned and walked away down Peach Street toward the town square. He wanted to see what was happening there. He had heard that Christmas Eve meant gatherings of people around the trees and lots of festive activities. Boy, was the radio right. The moment he turned the corner, he spotted the biggest tree he'd ever seen in his life. There were so many people walking around looking at lights, drinking hot chocolate, and saying "Merry Christmas" and "Happy Holidays" to each other.

"Merry Christmas," he said to a woman in a bright red coat as he walked past her.

"Thank you, Mr. Elf," she replied.

Toby looked through windows and saw the happiest of families exchanging gifts and singing songs. It made him think of his own family stuck down in the Marymount basement. Maybe it didn't matter where the family was as long as they were together. That's what it felt like, looking through the frosted windows of the houses in town. Caught up in his own mind, Toby was interrupted by a voice.

"Why are you walking around all alone dressed as an elf?"

Toby slowly turned and saw a teenage boy glaring at him with a smirk on his face. He didn't like how it made him feel.

"My family is back singing carols and I walked ahead of them," he said nervously.

"I think you look silly dressed like that," the teenager said. "Take off that gross mask."

Toby was scared. He wasn't wearing a mask, but the boy didn't know that.

"My mom made me this costume for Christmas," Toby replied. "I don't want to disappoint her."

"I said take it off," the boy said, coming toward him. "I don't like it."

Toby was very nervous and wasn't sure what to do. He recalled what Celeste had said to him when he went out for Halloween about not letting people scare him. But this boy was bigger and older than he was.

"I don't think you're being very Christmassy," Toby retorted, trying to gain back some courage.

"That's not even a word," the boy yelled. "Now give me that mask!"

Toby was frightened. As the boy came closer, he turned and ran. He ran past the carolers. He ran past the town Christmas tree. He ran until he saw the mansion in the distance. Toby didn't stop running until he had reached the backyard of Marymount Mansion.

Home.

Something that was familiar. A place where he felt safe. The boy hadn't followed him. He probably didn't even try to come after him. Toby stood there, breathing hard. Why had the boy been so nasty?

Toby wasn't hurting anyone by watching the families enjoy Christmas. Why did some people have to be mean for no reason?

Toby wiped away a tear that was trickling down his cold check. There was no way he could let anyone know what he had gone through. Perhaps he was done with exploring beyond the safe walls of the mansion. Once his tears were gone, he quietly made his way back inside the dark house.

7

I'm Not Scared

Toby had been silent for several days. Micaela was worried about her brother. After the other visits, he had come back to the basement so overjoyed. Not only didn't he bring her anything, but he had stayed by himself in the corner. Her mom had asked her if she knew what was wrong, but she kept her brother's secret. She didn't want him to get in trouble. Maybe he had learned his lesson and he wouldn't be going out in the world anymore. She thought it was time to talk to him about it. She walked over to the corner and sat down next to him, but didn't speak.

"Why are you staring at me?" Toby asked.

"I'm worried about you." Micaela said.

"You don't need to be, I'm fine," he gruffed.

"You haven't been the same ever since Christmas. What happened?"

Toby wasn't sure if he wanted to let his little sister know that there were mean people in the world. He wanted to protect her and allow her to live in the bubble that was their basement.

"Sometimes we find that things aren't what we expect when we get to them," Toby said.

"That's not very specific," Micaela replied.

Micaela was on to him, Toby realized.

She was a smarter little sister than he had given her credit for.

"This boy was picking on me, and it scared me," he said. "Which is weird, because people think that monsters are the scary ones."

"I'm not scared of monsters," Micaela said.

"Because you are a monster," Toby reminded her.

"Sometimes Mrs. Vanderpang can scare me."

"That's because she gets grumpy," he said. "You know she's really an old softie."

"I think people can be way more scary

than we are," Micaela said.

"How many people have you met?" Toby asked.

"Okay...that's a good point. I'm just going by a gut feeling."

Toby knew Micaela was right even though she hadn't seen many people. He had experienced some very welcoming people on Halloween and Thanksgiving. But it just took one to treat him differently and he ran. He was embarrassed that he had given in to fear so quickly, but he wasn't sure what that older boy might have done to him. Plus, he was scared of blowing the cover for his entire family as well as Ms. Celeste if anyone found out that she was helping his family. Toby was confused by it all now and not sure what he was going to do next. He had spent so much time thinking about the outside world that he had forgotten what his regular life was like.

"Are we going to drop an apple down the basement staircase at midnight on New Year's Eve?" Micaela asked.

Toby had started this tradition a few years earlier, and he and his little sister looked forward to it. The monsters would all cheer and talk about what they wanted to accomplish in the New Year. But how could anyone do anything when they were stuck in the same place day after day after day, Toby wondered.

"I'm not sure I'll be in the mood," he said.

Micaela hugged her brother tightly. She squeezed him until the entire space smelled of cotton candy.

"You're gonna make me pass out," Toby said.

"I just want you to know that I think I'm really lucky to have you as a brother," she announced as she walked away.

Toby had some decisions to make, but wasn't sure if he could make them alone. Should he talk to his mom? Ms. Celeste? Toby needed someone who had been around longer than he had and was wiser than him. Then it hit him.

Gwynasiam! He would have the answers!

8

Down the Long Chamber

Gwynasiam lived in the deepest, darkest part of the basement. He never came out to speak to the others. Some thought he was a myth passed down from generation to generation. The oldest monster in all of history—at least Toby's history. Toby had never actually seen him. He often wondered if he even existed. The mansion had different chambers in the basement, like different rooms, and there were parts that Toby and his family had never explored.

Toby had gotten so used to disappearing from his family to go outside, he figured they wouldn't miss him if he went off on an exploration of the basement. Surely if Gwynasiam was as wise as the elder monsters had said, he would have answers. Maybe he had tried to live out in the real world and would be able to give Toby some insight. Or what if Gwynasiam wasn't a friendly monster? How would

Toby react to that? He figured he had to take a shot and find out.

The morning after he had heard neighbors cheering in the New Year late into the night, he woke before anyone else and made his way down the long dark corridor that ran through the basement. He went past the point where all other monsters would turn back. All he could see was darkness, and he heard the dripping of water. *Ms. Celeste should know there is a leak in her basement*, he thought. He kept walking, slowly, until he saw the flicker of a candle. It had to be Gwynasiam's home. He heard the voice before he saw anything.

"Who is coming into my lair?"

"My name is Toby. I'm a monster too."

"No one comes down into this chamber," the voice boomed. "What makes you so brave?"

"My curiosity."

A large mass came looming out of the shadows and into the candlelight. There he was. Gwynasiam. A large purple monster with hair like a beastly lion's and tentacles like an octopus's. Toby's eyes widened. It was the largest monster he had ever seen.

"Gwynasiam?" he asked.

"It is I."

"Whoa. You are huge."

"Weren't you taught to be afraid of me?"

Gwynasiam asked.

"Monsters don't scare me," Toby stated. "People do."

Gwynasiam moved closer to Toby, slithering like a snake.

"You've seen people up close?" he asked.

"We see the woman who owns this mansion all the time," Toby said.

"And you're afraid of her?"

"Oh no. We love her and the people that work with her. My fear has come…"

"Go on," Gwynasiam said.

"I've snuck outside the mansion and wandered around in the real world. That's where I've met scarier humans."

Gwynasiam's entire body rose up as if he was about to strike, and then it all calmed down as he settled back on the basement floor. He looked deeply into Toby's eyes as he spoke.

"Monsters aren't meant to be with humans," Gwynasiam announced. "We are to stick to our own kind."

"Why?"

From Gwynasiam's silence and troubled look, Toby knew he had stumped the wise one who had lived for over one hundred years.

"Who has taught you to question so much, young monster?" Gwynasiam asked.

"I can't help but question and explore," Toby replied. "It's just something inside of me. I think we should be able to get along with others who aren't exactly like us."

"What brought you back to me?" Gwynasiam asked.

"I need someone older and wiser to tell me if I'm wrong. If just maybe there is another monster who feels the same way that I do."

Gwynasiam took a while before he replied.

"Many, many years ago I also went out into the world. Like you, I wanted to see what it was like. I found all kinds of people there, but all of them were afraid of me because I looked so different. They would run away screaming."

"I'm sorry you went through that," Toby said.

"Humans walk on two legs and I have all of these tentacles, so they assumed I was some monster from the sea,"

Gwynasiam said. "I realized then I would never be accepted. I don't even look like other monsters, so I slithered back here and have spent most of my life alone."

"That's so sad," Toby said. "Monsters would accept you. We don't care who looks different. I think you look pretty cool."

"Thank you, Toby."

Toby thought how hard it must be for Gwynasiam to have lived alone all these years, never speaking to anyone. He felt selfish for having a family who loved him and yet wanting to go out and meet new people when Gwynasiam was all by himself.

Toby held out his green paw to take one of Gwynasiam's tentacles.

"I think it's time you come back with me and meet the others," he declared.

9

Bringing Home a Prize

Toby felt like some famous explorer as he brought the legend that was Gwynasiam back to his part of the basement. He wasn't sure how his family would react, but hoped he wouldn't be in too much trouble. He saw his little sister as he entered the room, and his mom standing over her with a scowl on her face.

"Toby Moonboo Barghest!" Mom yelled.

All three names. Toby knew he was in trouble.

"Where have you been?" she finished.

"Mom, I needed some answers, and you've always said I should ask questions."

"You're not going to be able to—"

Mom couldn't even finish her sentence, because out of the shadows behind Toby came the largest monster he knew she had ever seen.

"Toby, get over here now!" she yelled with a frightened look on her face.

"Don't be scared, Mom," Toby said.

“This is Gwynasiam.”

The family all started to talk at once. Everyone had heard the stories of Gwynasiam throughout the years, but not one monster living in that basement had ever seen him.

Toby's dad stepped forward between Toby and Gwynasiam.

"Mr. Gwynasiam. We finally get to meet," he said.

"I haven't seen this part of the basement in decades," Gwynasiam said. "I love what you've done with the place."

The ease in Gwynasiam's voice made the family of monsters relax, and they welcomed him into their room.

"You must have some amazing stories to share," Toby's dad said.

"I've lived a very long life," Gwynasiam said. "But it's been a lonely one."

The monsters felt guilty that Gwynasiam

had spent so much time alone in a dark part of the basement.

"Can we get you something to eat?" Toby's mom asked.

"That would be lovely," Gwynasiam said. "Thank you."

The family brought him into the room, where he took up a huge portion of the space, and gave him some food.

"Had it not been for your son, Toby, I would still be back in that dark cell," Gwynasiam said.

"Toby, why did you go down there?" Toby's mom asked.

"Mom, I've done something you won't

be happy about," Toby said, bowing his head in shame.

"Mrs. Barghest, is it?" Gwynasiam asked.

"Yes," Toby's mom replied.

"You have one of the bravest sons I've ever met. His need to explore has helped me greatly."

"Toby, what else have you explored?" his dad asked.

"Well, since my Halloween outside, I've gone out a couple more times."

The monsters all began to chatter together, concern mixed with wonder over what Toby had experienced. Toby was a little overwhelmed by the number of questions being asked of him. Finally, his mom spoke up again.

"You broke the rules, Toby," she said. "You would have put Ms. Celeste in a tough place if anyone had found out."

"I honestly didn't mean to," Toby said. "But like Gwynasiam living alone, I wondered why we have to keep to ourselves down here. I imagined a world where monsters and humans could live together."

"That monster isn't thinking clearly," declared Mrs. Vanderpang from the corner.

"Toby, I'm not sure how many times we have to tell you that this is what is best for us," his mom said.

"But what if it's not," Toby replied. "What if there are people that would accept our differences and still want to be friends?"

"Like Ms. Celeste," Micaela said.

Toby smiled at his little sister. She was right. It had been there all along. Ms. Celeste was the perfect example of a human who loved the monsters and didn't care that they were different. If she could do it, maybe there were more.

"Your daughter makes a good point," Gwynasiam stated. The room went quiet again. "You've all been taken care of for all this time by a kind human who seems to really like you," Gwynasiam continued. "Surely she can't be the only one. I've spent a lifetime believing that monsters and people can't get along, and here you all were just down the corridor from me, proving me wrong every day."

Toby's mom let out a sigh. She knew they were all on to something.

"I've never thought of it that way, but I'm still upset you disobeyed us," she said to Toby.

"I'm so sorry, Mom. Can you ring the bell to call Ms. Celeste so I can apologize to her too?"

Mom smiled at her child, then went to the buzzer on the wall that the monsters used to notify Celeste when they needed her.

Ring. Ring. Ring.

10

The Monster in the Sun

Celeste stood in the middle of all the monsters as they made their case. Toby apologized over and over. Ms. Celeste seemed a little stunned by the size of Gwynasiam, but she would learn he was a big teddy bear. She listened to each of them and then turned to Toby.

"Toby, what did you learn when you were outside?" she asked.

"There are nice people and there are mean people," he said. "There are families that love each other just like us. People are merry around holidays, and some people can't help but bully others."

"That all sounds about right," Celeste said.

"So what happens now?" Toby's mom asked.

Toby went to the window at the top of the basement wall and looked out at the moon.

"My last trip, I got so scared and ran

home," he said. "But then I went to see Gwynasiam and realized I wasn't scared of him when I didn't know him. So I think it's time I try something else that I've not done."

Everyone began to guess what Toby might mean.

"You mean take me with you?" Micaela asked.

"You're still too young," Toby said. "We need to wait until you're eight, the way Ms. Celeste and Mom did with me."

"Rats!" Micaela yelled.

"But I think it's time I go outside without a costume on, during the daylight."

"I don't know how I feel about that," Toby's mom said.

Toby's dad looked at Gwynasiam, who gave a nod. He looked at Celeste, who smiled. Finally, Dad spoke.

"I think Toby has proved himself to this family," he announced. "He has brought someone back to us that we didn't even know we missed. It's time. Let the young monster try this quest."

Mom looked at all the monsters around the room waiting for her approval.

"Ms. Celeste," she said. "Do you agree?"

"I do."

"Then it's set. Toby will go out tomorrow morning and see what waits for him."

At that, the monsters cheered. Celeste gave Toby a big squeeze, causing the scent of cotton candy to spray around the room.

"There it is again, that smell that I love," Celeste said. "Toby, if you can do this, then I should be able to tell the humans in my life the secret I've been carrying."

"You're gonna tell Ms. Margaret and Mr. Rick?" Micaela asked.

"Yes, Micaela," Celeste said. "If Toby can be brave, so can I. Who knows…I bet there are two more humans that will enjoy the company of all of you."

Micaela hugged Celeste before she turned and went up the stairs.

Toby squeezed his mom and then went to his corner to rest. He knew he wouldn't be getting much sleep that night.

When the sun came up, the monsters were all waiting at the top of the staircase for Celeste. The door opened, and there stood Margaret and Rick.

"Good morning to you all," Margaret said with a look of shock on her face.

"Hello, Ms. Margaret," Toby replied. "I've been hearing your voice for years. It's so great to meet you face to face."

Celeste stepped forward from behind the two, waving them all in.

"Let's not stand here at the basement door," she said. "It's time to get Toby outside on his adventure."

Everyone followed Celeste to the mansion's front door and squeezed in to watch Toby walk out into the sun. He stepped on one of the porch boards that made the squeaking noise.

"Mr. Rick, maybe I can help you fix this someday," Toby said.

"I would love that, Toby," Rick said, with only a little hesitation.

"I would say don't talk to strangers, but that's why you're venturing out," Celeste said.

"I want you to enjoy yourself, son," Toby's mom reminded him. "Know that we all love you."

"I know," Toby said. "Thank you for letting me do this."

With a few hugs and a wave goodbye, Toby started down the front walk without wearing a costume.

The first thing he noticed was the feeling of the sun on his arm. It was soothing, its warmth taking the edge off the chilly day. It made his fur tingle. He saw a big yellow bus full of kids who he figured were off to school. He saw a crossing guard stopping traffic with a big red sign to let people walk across the street. He waved to a mailman who was delivering mail around the neighborhood. He swore he recognized a few kids that he had gone trick-or-treating with, but couldn't really tell since they were out of their costumes. He then saw a group of moms who had just walked their kids to school across the street.

"Look at that odd creature," one announced as she pointed at Toby.

Toby became slightly nervous that they might approach him and question him.

"Kids today," another said. "You never

know how they're gonna dress anymore."

With that, the ladies walked away.

Whew! Toby had thought for sure they would run over and attack him, but they hadn't. He was still walking, breathing in the fresh air, and he felt amazing.

Toby walked along Main Street, looking into the houses and stores. Everything seemed different during the day than when he had been out at night. At one point, he saw his reflection in a window and stopped.

He really did look different from all the humans. Just like Gwynasiam looked so different from his monster family. But then he noticed the people. Some had darker skin, while others had lighter skin. They all dressed differently. Some wore glasses. The more he looked, the more he noticed that no two were exactly the same.

He sat down under a tree to watch people walk by. He picked a few dandelions left over from fall while he looked at the different sorts of animals they had with them. Dogs, cats...someone was even walking a baby pig on a leash. Toby laughed when a dog barked at him, and he barked back.

So many people just walked past him without thinking anything of a monster sitting under a tree. Then a man came over.

"Are you lost?" the man asked. "Do you need help finding your way home on this winter day?"

Toby noticed the man wasn't treating him any differently from the other humans. He was being kind and thoughtful.

"I think I'm gonna be okay," Toby

declared. "Thank you."

The man took off his glove, reached out to shake Toby's hand. Toby saw how different his monster arm looked next to the human one. He took the man's hand and shook it.

"Have a great day, young man," the man said, and walked away.

Young man, Toby thought. He had called him human. Toby realized what a huge moment this had been. But he didn't want to push his luck, as he wanted to be home by lunchtime. He got up and walked back toward the mansion with pride in his step and his head spinning. He had discovered so much in such a short amount of time.

Sure, he might continue living in that basement until he was old enough to move out on his own, but he would no longer feel the need to hide who he truly was from the rest of the world. Toby looked up and saw his family waiting on the porch with Ms. Celeste and their other two human friends. It seemed his curiosity had rubbed off on the others as each of them had taken a moment in the sun as well. He knew they would have so much to talk about over lunch with Ms. Celeste.

"Welcome home, Toby," Ms. Celeste

shouted as he came up the steps.

"Mrs. Vanderpang, I picked this for you," Toby said, and handed her a dandelion.

Mrs. Vanderpang smiled and blew into the dandelion, watching the pieces float into the air.

"I've always wanted to do that," she said.

Toby's mom put her arm around Mrs. Vanderpang to lead her into the house. Micaela yanked on her brother's hand to pull him inside. As the monsters neared the basement door, Celeste spoke up.

"Wait!" she yelled. "In here. The fireplace is going, let's all get warm."

Celeste pointed to the main parlor. The monsters all smiled, then ran into the front room and crowded around Toby as they yelled out questions about his day. Gwynasiam took up most of the parlor with his huge tentacles.

"It was amazing," Toby declared as he jumped up on the fireplace hearth. "Now sit back, and I'll tell you all the adventures I had out in the world."

THE END

About the Author

Gregory G. Allen is an award-winning author, screenwriter, filmmaker and actor. His children's books include Chicken Boy: The Adventures of a Superhero with Autism, Chicken Boy Deals with Doctors & Dentists, and Irving the Theater Nut! He is a member of The Society of Children's Book Writers and Illustrators and The Dramatist Guild. The idea for his monster book goes back to the first musical he ever wrote which was produced for the stage when he was 15 with the message that it's ok to be different.

gregsimagination.com

About the Illustrator

Shelby Goodwin is an illustrator, letterer, graphic designer, and all-around creative living in Hoboken, NJ. She is extremely passionate about children's media and the power of art to romanticize the everyday. When she is not making things, she can be found with her spouse and three cats exploring new places, eating pastries, or cuddling up in her favorite reading chair.

heartonmysleevedesign.com

Printed in the USA
CPSIA information can be obtained
at www.ICGtesting.com
LVHW040422101023
760559LV00023B/119